River Rescue!

EGMONT
We bring stories to life

First published in Great Britain 2008
by Egmont UK Limited, 239 Kensington High Street, London W8 6SA
© 2008 Prism Art & Design Limited, a HIT Entertainment company.
Based on an original idea by D. Gingell, D. Jones and characters created by R. M. J. Lee.
The Fireman Sam name and character are trademarks of Prism Art & Design Limited,
a HIT Entertainment company.

ISBN 978 1 4052 3812 0
1 3 5 7 9 10 8 6 4 2
Printed in Singapore

One day, Fireman Sam was fixing a puncture in one of Jupiter's tyres when Elvis came along.

"Need any help, Sam?" asked Elvis, eagerly. "I'm great at fixing punctures."

"No thanks, Elvis," smiled Sam. "I think I've got everything under control."

Elvis looked very disappointed. But just then, James and Sarah arrived, carrying a deflated beach ball.

"Rosa just stuck her claws in our beach ball," said James. "Can you fix it?"

"I'll do it! I'll do it!" said Elvis, quickly perking up, and going to get his puncture repair kit.

In the countryside, Tom Thomas was expertly flying a kite. Norman and Mandy were watching in admiration.

"Cor, that's a cool kite, Tom. Can I borrow it?" asked Norman.

"Sure, as long as you're careful with it," replied Tom, winding in the kite by tugging on the line.

"Careful's my middle name!" said Norman, as Tom handed him the kite.

Mandy looked at him in disbelief.

At the Fire Station, Elvis had repaired the puncture, but he'd also got the ball glued to his hand!

"Going through a sticky patch, I see, Cridlington!" laughed Station Officer Steele.

"Yes, Sir. Very funny, Sir," replied Elvis.

"Now, men," said Officer Steele. "This sunshine will have people out on the water, so we need to check our safety equipment."

"The pontoon in particular," added Sam. "It's a sort of airbed for rescues on water," he explained to the twins.

But when Officer Steele went to get it from Jupiter's locker, the pontoon wasn't there.

"I put it in a safe place," said Elvis. "Though it's so safe, I can't quite remember where it is . . ."

Outside Dilys' shop, Norman and Mandy were looking at the kite. Norman was wearing his skateboarding helmet and knee pads, and had a full bag of newspapers over his shoulder.

"Are you sure about this?" asked Mandy.

"Yeah, with this little baby, I'll be able to do my newspaper round twice as fast!" replied Norman, clutching the kite to his chest. "See you later, Mandy!"

Then Norman tossed the kite in the air and held on to the line.

"Hey, wait for me!" shouted Mandy, running after him.

Norman was going faster and faster on his skateboard, as the wind tugged at the kite.

"Here comes the fastest paper boy in the world," he shouted.

When Norman reached Bella's café, he threw her newspaper at the door.

"Mamma Mia!" cried Bella, looking outside.

"Flaming koalas!" said Tom.

"Norman, what on earth are you doing . . .!?" asked Dilys.

"Express delivery, Mam," said Norman, before he sped off.

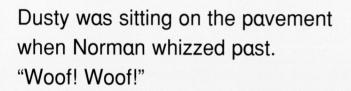

Dusty was sitting on the pavement
when Norman whizzed past.
"Woof! Woof!"

Then the kite pulled Norman into the road,
as Trevor was driving up the street!

The bus screeched to a halt, and Norman managed to get safely
out of the way just in time.

"Goodness gracious, Norman's gone supersonic! If he's not
careful, he'll have an accident," said Trevor.

Around the corner, Sarah and James were bouncing their ball.

"Hi, have you seen Norman?" asked Mandy.

The twins shook their heads.

"If you do, get out of the way!" laughed Mandy and off she went.

But just then, they heard Norman approaching – "Wheee!"

"Look out, James!" shouted Sarah.

James jumped out of Norman's path just in time.

Norman sped straight past on his skateboard, then skidded out of control towards the lake.

"Aaargh! Aaargh! Oooh!" he cried, as a big gust of wind caught the kite and lifted Norman over the lake.

The wind dropped and Norman plunged into the water with a loud splash!

"Oh no!" cried Sarah and James. "Norman can't swim!"

At the Fire Station, Elvis had finally found the pontoon, but he quickly discovered that it had a puncture! Elvis tried to repair it, but he glued more rubber patches to himself than the pontoon! With Sam's help, it was soon repaired.

Back at the lake, Norman was struggling in the water.

"We'd better get Uncle Sam," said Sarah.

"You go, I'll stay here," said James. And Sarah ran for help.

"Ah! Ah!" shouted Norman.

"Grab hold of this, Norman," said James and he threw him the beach ball.

But it landed out of Norman's reach!

Sarah's emergency message quickly reached the Fire Station.

"Oh no! Norman Price has been blown into the lake," said Sam.

"Scramble, men. Action Stations!" said Station Officer Steele.

Sam and Elvis put the inflatable pontoon in Jupiter's locker and the Fire Crew were ready. Jupiter's lights began to flash and the siren wailed, Nee Nah! Nee Nah!

Penny and Venus set off close behind.

At the lake, Norman was trying to keep his head above water.

"Help! Help!" he gasped.

"Norman, turn on to your back and kick," shouted James.

"I'll try," gasped Norman, and he turned and started kicking.

"Head for that little island," said James.

And Norman turned his head to find a rock in the middle of the lake, and then kicked his way to it.

Just then, they heard Jupiter's siren. Nee Nah! Nee Nah!

"It's OK, Uncle Sam's coming. He'll save you!" said James.

Jupiter and Venus arrived at the lake with the Fire Crew.

"He's over there, Uncle Sam," said James.

"Yes, we see him, James," replied Sam.

"Inflate the pontoon, men!' said Station Officer Steele.

And Sam and Elvis unloaded the pontoon and Penny plugged it into Jupiter's generator.

"Pontoon inflated, Sir," said Penny.

"We'll soon have you out of there, Norman!" said Sam.

Fireman Sam took his first swaying step on the inflatable pontoon towards Norman.

"Cor, that's just like the bouncy castle we had at Mandy's birthday party!" said Sarah, admiring the pontoon.

The wind suddenly picked up, swaying the pontoon, and Sam was nearly knocked off balance!

"Wo-ow. Steady there. You alright?" asked Penny, anxiously, catching her breath.

"Yes, I'm fine, Penny," replied Sam, giving her the thumbs up.

"Hurry up, Sam. I think a fish has just swum up my trouser leg!" said Norman, as he clung to the rock.

Sam managed to lift Norman on to the pontoon.

"Hold on tight, Norman," said Sam.

"Thanks, Sam," replied Norman, quietly.

Sam carefully carried Norman to safety, as the pontoon swayed.

"Well done, Sam. First class operation," said Officer Steele, as Sam put Norman down on the bank.

Then Norman pulled a wriggling fish out of his jeans and threw it back into the lake!

Dilys and Mandy were waiting outside the shop when they all got back.

"Norman, thank heavens you're safe. I thought I'd never see your little freckled face again!" cried Dilys.

"I've gone off kite-flying, Mam," said Norman.

"There's nothing wrong with flying a kite, Norman. Just make sure you take care," said Sam.

"OK, Sam," said Norman. "But I'm going to learn to swim."

"You've got to learn to float first," said Dilys, giving him some arm bands. "Come on, you can try these out in a nice hot bath."

"Oh, Mam!" said Norman, as Dilys pulled him into the shop.

And everyone laughed!

Stay Safe!

Can you remember what to do if a fire breaks out?

Get out.
Get the Fire Brigade out.
Stay out!

Sam's Safety Tips

 Never play with matches or lighters.

 If you smell smoke or see fire, tell a grown-up.

 Don't play near hot ovens, or boiling pots and pans.

 Keep toys and clothes away from fires and heaters.

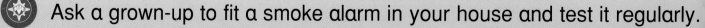 Ask a grown-up to fit a smoke alarm in your house and test it regularly.